A Night in Rome

William Harrison Ainsworth

A Night in Rome

By

William Harrison Ainsworth

1856

The Pope was saying the high, high mass.
All on Saint Peter's day;
With the power to him given by the saints in heaven.
To wash men's sins away.

The Pope he was saying the blessed mass.
And the people kneel'd around;
And from each man's soul his sins did pass. As he kissed the holy ground.

The Grey Brother

I. Santa Maria Maggiore

Chancing to be in Rome in the August of 1830, I visited the gorgeous church of Santa Maria Maggiore during the celebration of the anniversary of the Holy Assumption.

It was a glorious sight to one unaccustomed to the imposing religious ceremonials of the Romish church, to witness all the pomp and splendour displayed at this high solemnity—to gaze down that glittering pile, and mark the various ecclesiastical dignitaries, each in their peculiar and characteristic costume, employed in the ministration of their sacred functions, and surrounded by a wide semicircle of the papal guards, so stationed to keep back the crowd, and who, with their showy scarlet attire and tall halberds, looked like the martial figures we see in the sketches of Callot. Nor was the brilliant effect of this picture diminished by the sumptuous framework in which it was set. Overhead flamed a roof resplendent with burnished gold; before me rose a canopy supported by pillars of porphyry, and shining with many-coloured stones; while on either hand were chapels devoted to some noble house, and boasting each the marble memorial of a pope. Melodious masses proper to the service were ever and anon chanted by the papal choir, and overpowering perfume was diffused around by a hundred censers.

Subdued by the odours, the music, and the spectacle, I sank into a state of dreamy enthusiasm, during a continuance of which I almost fancied myself a convert to the faith of Rome, and surrendered myself unreflectingly to an admiration of its errors. As I gazed among the surrounding crowd, the sight of so many prostrate figures, all in attitudes of deepest devotion, satisfied me of the profound religious impression of the ceremonial. As elsewhere; this feeling was not universal; and, as elsewhere, likewise, more zeal was exhibited by the lower than the higher classes of society; and I occasionally noted amongst the latter the glitter of an eye or the flutter of a bosom, not altogether agitated; I suspect; by holy aspirations. Yet me thought, on the whole, I had never seen such abandonment of soul, such prostration of spirit, in my own colder clime, and during the exercise of my own more chastened creed, as that which in several instances I now beheld; and I almost envied the poor maiden near me, who, abject upon the earth, had washed away her sorrows, and perhaps her sins, in contrite tears.

As such thoughts swept through my mind, I felt a pleasure in singling out particular figures and groups which interested me, from their peculiarity of costume, or from their devotional fervour. Amongst others, a little to my left, I remarked a band of mountaineers from Calabria, for such I judged them to be from their wild and picturesque garb. Deeply was every individual of this little knot of peasantry impressed by the ceremonial. Every eye was humbly cast down; every knee bent; every hand was either occupied in grasping the little crucifix suspended from its owner's neck, in telling the beads of his rosary, or fervently crossed upon his bare and swarthy breast.

While gazing upon this group, I chanced upon an individual whom I had not hitherto noticed; and who now irresistibly attracted my attention. Though a little removed from the Calabrian mountaineers, and reclining against the marble walls of the church, he evidently belonged to the same company; at least, so his attire seemed to indicate, though the noble cast of his countenance was far superior to that of his comrades. He was an old man, with a face of the fine antique Roman stamp—a bold outline of prominent nose, rugged and imperious brow, and proudly-cut chin. His head and chin, as well as his naked breast, were frosted over with the snowy honours of many winters, and their hoar appearance contrasted strikingly with the tawny hue of a skin almost as dark and as lustrous as polished oak. Peasant as he was, there was something of grandeur and majesty in this old man's demeanour and physiognomy. His head declined backwards, so as completely to expose his long and muscular throat. His arms hung listlessly by his side; one hand drooped upon the pavement, the other was placed within his breast: his eyes were closed. The old man's garb was of the coarsest fabric; he wore little beyond a shirt, a loose vest, a sort of sheep-skin cloak, and canvas leggings bound around with leathern thongs. His appearance, however, was above his condition; he became his rags as proudly as a prince would have become his ermined robe.

The more I scrutinised the rigid lines of this old man's countenance, the more I became satisfied that many singular, and perhaps not wholly guiltless, events were connected with his history. The rosary was in his hand—the cross upon his breast—the beads were untold—the crucifix unclasped—no breath of prayer passed his lips. His face was turned heavenward, but his eyes were closed, —he dared not open them. Why did he come thither, if he did not venture to pray Why did he assume a penitential attitude, if he felt no penitence?

So absorbed was I in the perusal of the workings of this old man's countenance, as to be scarcely conscious that the service of high mass was concluded, and the crowd within the holy pile fast dispersing. The music was hushed, the robed prelates and their train had disappeared, joyous dames were hastening along the marble aisles to their equipages; all, save a few kneeling figures near the chapels, were departing; and the old man, aware, from the stir and hum prevailing around, that the ceremonial was at an end, arose, stretched out his arm to one of his comrades, a youth who had joined him, and prepared to follow the concourse.

Was he really blind? Assuredly not. Besides, he did not walk like as one habituated to the direst calamity that can befal our nature. He staggered in his gait, and reeled to and fro. Yet wherefore did he not venture to unclose his eyes within the temple of the Most High? What would I not have given to be made acquainted with his history! For I felt that it must be a singular one. I might satisfy my curiosity at once. He was moving slowly forward, guided by his comrade. In a few seconds it would be too late—he would have vanished from my sight. With hasty footsteps I followed him down the church, and laid my hand, with some violence, upon his shoulder.

The old man started at the touch, and turned. Now, indeed, his eyes were opened wide, and flashing full upon me, —and such eyes! Heretofore I had only dreamed of such. Age had not quenched their lightning, and I quailed beneath the fierce glances which he threw upon me. But if I was, at first, surprised at the display of anger which I had called forth in him, how much more was I astonished to behold the whole expression of his countenance suddenly change. His eyes continued fixed upon mine as if I had been a basilisk. Apparently he could not avert them; while his whole frame shivered with emotion. I advanced towards him; he shrank backwards, and, but for the timely aid of his companion, would have fallen upon the pavement.

At a loss to conceive in what way I could have occasioned him so much alarm, I rushed forward to the assistance of the old man, when his son, for such it subsequently appeared he was, rudely repelled me, and thrust his hand into his girdle; as if to seek for means to prevent further interference.

Meanwhile the group had been increased by the arrival of a third party, attracted by the cry the old man had uttered in falling. The new comer was an Italian gentleman, somewhat stricken in year; of stern and stately deportment, and with something sinister and forbidding in his aspect. He was hastening towards the old man, but he suddenly stopped, and was about to retire when he encountered my gaze. As our eyes met he started; and a terror, as sudden and lively as that exhibited by the old man, was at once depicted in his features.

My surprise was now beyond all bounds, and I continued for some moments speechless with astonishment. Not a little of the inexplicable awe which affected the old man and the stranger was communicated to myself. Altogether, we formed a mysterious and terrible triangle of which each side bore some strange and unintelligible relation to the other.

The new comer first recovered his composure, though not without an effort. Coldly turning his heel upon me, he walked towards the old man, and shook him forcibly. The latter shrank from his grasp, and endeavoured to avoid him; but it was impossible. The stranger whispered a few words in his ear, of which, from his gestures being directed towards myself, I could guess the import. The old man replied. His action in doing so was that of supplication and despair. The stranger retorted in a wild and vehement manner, and even stamped his foot upon the ground; but the old man still continued to cling to the knees of his superior.

"Weak, superstitious fool! " at length exclaimed the stranger, "I will waste no more words upon thee. Do, or say, what thou wilt; but beware! " And spurning him haughtily back with his foot, he strode away.

The old man's reverend head struck against the marble floor. His temple was cut open by the fall, and blood gushed in torrents from the wound. Recovering himself, he started to his feet—a knife was instantly in his hand, and he would have pursued and doubtless slain his aggressor, if he had not been forcibly withheld by his son, and by a priest who had joined them.

"Maledizione! " exclaimed the old man—"a blow from him—from that hand! I will stab him, though he were at the altar's foot; though he had a thousand lives, each should pay for it. Release me, Paolo! release me! for, by Heaven! he dies! "

"Peace, father! " cried the son, still struggling with him.

"Thou art not my son, to hinder my revenge! " shouted the enraged father. "Dost not see this blood—my blood—thy father's blood? —and thou holdest me back? Thou shouldst have struck him to the earth for the deed—but he was a noble, and thou daredst not lift thy hand against him! "

"Wouldst thou have had me slay him in this holy place? " exclaimed Paolo, reddening with anger and suppressed emotion.

"No, no, " returned the old man, in an altered voice; "not here, not here, though 'twere but just retribution. But I will find other means of vengeance. I will denounce him—I will betray all, though it cost me my own life! He shall die by the hands of the common executioner; — there is one shall testify for me! " And he pointed to me.

Again I advanced towards him.

"If thou hast aught to disclose pertaining to the Holy Church, I am ready to listen to thee, my son, " said the priest; "but reflect well ere thou bringest any charge thou mayest not be able to substantiate against one who stands so high in her esteem as him thou wouldst accuse. "

The son gave his father a meaning look, and whispered somewhat in his ear. The old man became suddenly still.

"Right, right, " said he; "I have bethought me. 'Twas but a blow. He is wealthy, I am poor; there is no justice for the poor in Rome. "

"My purse is at your service, " said I, interfering; "you shall have my aid. "

"Your aid! " echoed the old man, staring at me; "will you assist me, signor? "

"I will. "

"Enough. I may claim fulfilment of your promise. "

"Stop, old man, " I said; "answer me one question ere you depart. Whence arose your recent terrors. "

"You shall know hereafter, signor, " he said; "I must now begone. We shall meet again. Follow me not, " he continued, seeing I was bent upon obtaining further explanation of the mystery. "You will learn nothing now, and only endanger my safety. Addio, signor. " And with hasty steps he quitted the church, accompanied by his son.

"Who is that old man? " I demanded of the priest.

"I am as ignorant as yourself, " he replied, "but he must be looked to; he talks threateningly. " And he beckoned to an attendant.

"Who was he who struck him? " was my next inquiry.

"One of our wealthiest nobles, " he replied, "and an assured friend of the church. We could ill spare him. Do not lose sight of them, " he added to the attendant, "and let the sbirri track them to their haunts. They must not be suffered to go forth to-night. A few hours' restraint will cool their hot Calabrian blood. "

"But the name of the noble, father? " I said, renewing my inquiries.

"I must decline further questioning, " returned the priest, coldly. "I have other occupation; and meanwhile it will be well to have these stains effaced, which may else bring scandal on these holy walls. You will excuse me, my son. " So saying, he bowed and retired.

I made fruitless inquiries for the old man at the door of the church. He was gone; none of the bystanders who had seen him go forth knew whither.

Stung by curiosity, I wandered amid the most unfrequented quarters of Rome throughout the day, in the hope of meeting with the old Calabrian, but in vain. As, however, I entered the court-yard of my hotel, I fancied I discovered, amongst the lounging assemblage gathered round the door, the dark eyes of the younger mountaineer. In this I might have been mistaken. No one answering to his description had been seen near the house.

II. The Marchesa

Une chose ténébreuse fait par des hommes ténébreux. —Lucrece Borgia.

On the same night I bent my steps towards the Colosseum; and, full of my adventure of the morning, found myself, not without apprehension, involved within its labyrinthine passages. Accompanied by a monk, who, with a small horn lantern in his hand, acted as my guide, I fancied that, by its uncertain light, I could discover stealthy figures lurking within the shades of the ruin.

Whatever suspicions I might entertain, I pursued my course in silence. Emerging from the vomitorio, we stood upon the steps of the colossal amphitheatre. The huge pile was bathed in rosy moonlight, and reared itself in serene majesty before my view.

While indulging in a thousand speculations, occasioned by the hour and the spot, I suddenly perceived a figure on a point of the ruin immediately above me. Nothing but the head was visible; but that was placed in bold relief against the beaming sky of night, and I recognised it at once. No nobler Roman head had ever graced the circus when Rome was in her zenith. I shouted to the old Calabrian, for he it was I beheld. Almost ere the sound had left my lips, he had disappeared. I made known what I had seen to the monk. He was alarmed—urged our instant departure, and advised me to seek the assistance of the sentinel stationed at the entrance to the pile. To this proposal I assented; and, having descended the vasty steps and crossed the open arena, we arrived, without molestation, at the doorway.

The sentinel had allowed no one to pass him. He returned with me to the circus; and, after an ineffectual search amongst the ruins, volunteered his services to accompany me homewards through the Forum. I declined his offer, and shaped my course towards a lonesome vicolo on the right. This was courting danger; but I cared not, and walked slowly forward through the deserted place.

Scarcely had I proceeded many paces, when I heard footsteps swiftly approaching; and, ere I could turn round, my arms were seized from behind, and a bandage was passed across my eyes. All my efforts at liberation were unavailing; and, after a brief struggle, I remained passive.

"Make no noise, " said a voice which I knew to be that of the old man, "and no harm shall befal you. You must come with us. Ask no questions, but follow. "

A Night In Rome

I suffered myself to be led, without further opposition whithersoever they listed. We walked for it might be half an hour, much beyond the walls of Rome. I had to scramble through many ruins and frequently stumbled over inequalities of ground. I now felt the fresh breeze of night blowing over the wide campagna, and my conductors moved swiftly onwards as we trod on its elastic turf.

At length they came to a halt. My bandage was removed, and I beheld myself beneath the arch of an aqueduct, which spanned the moonlit plain. A fire was kindled beneath the arch, and the ruddy flame licked its walls. Around the blaze were grouped the little band of peasantry I had beheld within the church, in various and picturesque attitudes. They greeted my conductors on their arrival, and glanced inquisitively at me, but did not speak to me. The elder Calabrian, whom they addressed as Cristofano, asked for a glass of aqua vitae, which he handed respectfully to me. I declined the offer, but he pressed it upon me.

"You will need it, Signor, " he said; "you have much to do to-night. You fear, perhaps, it is drugged. Behold! " And he drank it off.

I could not, after this, refuse his pledge. "And now, signor, " said the old man, removing to a little distance from the group, "may I crave a word with you—your name? "

As I had no reason for withholding it, I told him how I was called.

"Hum! Had you no relation of the name of—-"

"None whatever. " And I sighed, for I thought of my desolate condition.

"Strange! " he muttered; adding, with a grim smile, "but, however, likenesses are easily accounted for. "

"What likenesses? " I asked. "Whom do I resemble? and what is the motive of your inexplicable conduct?"

"You shall hear, " he replied, frowning gloomily. "Step aside, and let us get within the shade of these arches, out of the reach of yonder listeners. The tale I have to tell is for your ears alone. "

I obeyed him; and we stood beneath the shadow of the aqueduct.

"Years ago, " began the old man, "an Englishman, in all respects resembling yourself; equally well-favoured in person, and equally young, came to

A Night In Rome

Rome, and took up his abode within the eternal city. He was of high rank in his own country, and was treated with the distinction due to his exalted station here. At that time I dwelt with the Marchese di—-. I was his confidential servant—his adviser—his friend. I had lived with his father—carried him as an infant—sported with him as a boy—loved and served him as a man. Loved him, I say; for, despite his treatment of me, I loved him then as much as I abhor him now. Well! signor, to my story. If his youth had been profligate, his manhood was not less depraved; it was devoted to cold, calculating libertinism. Soon after he succeeded to the estates and title of his father, he married. That he loved his bride, I can scarcely believe; for, though he was wildly jealous of her, he was himself unfaithful, and she knew it. In Italy, revenge, in such cases; is easily within a woman's power; and, for aught I know, the marchesa might have meditated retaliation. My lord, however, took the alarm, and thought fit to retire to his villa without the city, and for a time remained secluded within its walls. It was at this crisis that the Englishman I have before mentioned arrived in Rome. My lady, who mingled little with the gaieties of the city, had not beheld him; but she could not have been unacquainted with him by report, as every tongue was loud in his praises. A rumour of his successes with other dames had reached my lord; nay, I have reason to believe that he had been thwarted by the handsome Englishman in some other quarter, and he sedulously prevented their meeting. An interview, however, did take place between them, and in an unexpected manner. It was the custom then, as now, upon particular occasions, to drive, during the heats of summer, within the Piazza Navona, which is flooded with water. One evening the marchesa drove thither: she was unattended, except by myself. Our carriage happened to be stationed near that of the young Englishman. "

"The marchesa was beautiful, no doubt? " I said, interrupting him.

"Most beautiful! " he replied; "and so your countryman seemed to think, for he was lost in admiration of her. I am not much versed in the language of the eyes, but his were too eloquent and expressive not to be understood. I watched my mistress narrowly. It was evident from her glowing cheek, though her eyes were cast down, that she was not insensible to his regards. She turned to play with her dog, a lovely little greyhound, which was in the carriage beside her, and patted it carelessly with the glove which she held in her hand. The animal snatched the glove from her grasp, and, as he bounded backwards, fell over the carriage side. My lady uttered a scream at the sight, and I was preparing to extricate the struggling dog, when the Englishman plunged into the water. In an instant he had restored her favourite to the marchesa, and received her warmest acknowledgments. From that moment an intimacy commenced, which was destined to produce the most fatal consequences to both parties. "

"Did you betray them? " I asked, somewhat impatiently.

"I was then the blind tool of the marchese. I did so, " replied the old man. "I told him all particulars of the interview. He heard me in silence, but grew ashy pale with suppressed rage. Bidding me redouble my vigilance, he left me. My lady was now scarcely ever out of my sight; when one evening, a few days after what had occurred, she walked forth alone upon the garden-terrace of the villa. Her guitar was in her hand, and her favourite dog by her side. I was at a little distance, but wholly unperceived. She struck a few plaintive chords upon her instrument, and then, resting her chin upon her white and rounded arm, seemed lost in tender reverie. Would you had seen her, signor, as I beheld her then, or as one other beheld her! you would acknowledge that you had never met with her equal in beauty. Her raven hair fell in thick tresses over shoulders of dazzling whiteness and the most perfect proportion. Her deep dark eyes were thrown languidly on the ground, and her radiant features were charged with an expression of profound and pensive passion.

"In this musing attitude she continued for some minutes, when she was aroused by the gambols of her dog, who bore in his mouth a glove which he had found. As she took it from him, a letter dropped upon the floor. Had a serpent glided from its folds, it could not have startled her more. She gazed upon the paper, offended, but irresolute. Yes, she was irresolute; and you may conjecture the rest. She paused, and by that pause was lost. With a shrinking grasp she stooped to raise the letter. Her cheeks, which had grown deathly pale, again kindled with blushes as she perused it. She hesitated—cast a bewildering look towards the mansion—placed the note within her bosom—and plunged into the orange-bower. "

"Her lover awaited her there? "

"He did. I saw them meet. I heard his frenzied words—his passionate entreaties. He urged her to fly—she resisted. He grew more urgent— more impassioned. She uttered a faint cry, and I stood before them. The Englishman's hand was at my throat, and his sword at my breast, with the swiftness of thought; and but for the screams of my mistress, that instant must have been my last. At her desire he relinquished his hold of me; but her cries had reached other ears, and the marchese arrived to avenge his injured honour. He paused not to inquire the nature of the offence, but, sword in hand, assailed the Englishman, bidding me remove his lady. The clash of their steel was drowned by her shrieks as I bore her away; but I knew the strife was desperate. Before I gained the house my lady had fainted; and, committing her to the charge of other attendants, I returned to the terrace. I met my master slowly walking homewards. His sword was gone—his brow was bent—he shunned my sight. I knew what had happened, and did not approach him. He sought his wife. What passed in that interview was never disclosed, but it may be guessed at from its result. That night the marchesa left her husband's halls—never to return. Next morn I visited the terrace where she had received the token. The glove was still upon the ground. I picked it up and carried it to the marchese, detailing the whole occurrence to him. He took it, and vowed as he took it that his vengeance should never rest satisfied till that glove had been steeped in her blood. "

"And he kept his vow? " I asked, shuddering.

"Many months elapsed ere its accomplishment. Italian vengeance is slow, but sure. To all outward appearance, he had forgotten his faithless wife. He had even formed a friendship with her lover, which he did the more effectually to blind his ultimate designs. Meanwhile, time rolled on, and the marchesa gave birth to a child—the offspring of her seducer. "

"Great God! " I exclaimed, "was that child a boy? "

"It was—but listen to me. My tale draws to a close. One night, during the absence of the Englishman, by secret means we entered the palazzo where the marchesa resided. We wandered from room to room till we came to her chamber. She was sleeping, with her infant by her side. The sight maddened the marchese. He would have stricken the child, but I held back his hand. He relented. He bade me make fast the door. He approached the bed. I heard a rustle—a scream. A white figure sprang from out the couch. In an instant the light was extinguished—there was a blow—another—and all was over. I threw open the door. The marchese came forth, The corridor in which we stood was flooded with moonlight. A glove was in his hand—it was dripping with blood. His oath was fulfilled—his vengeance complete—no, not complete, for the Englishman yet lived. "

"What became of him? " I inquired.

"Ask me not, " replied the old man; "you were at the Chiesa Santa Maria Maggiore this morning. If those stones could speak, they might tell a fearful story. "

"And that was the reason you did not dare to unclose your eyes within those holy precincts—a film of blood floated between you and heaven. "

The old man shuddered, but replied not.

"And the child? " I asked, after a pause; "what of their wretched offspring? "

"It was conveyed to England by a friend of its dead father. If he were alive, that boy would be about your age, signor. "

"Indeed! " I said; a horrible suspicion flashing across my mind.

"After the Englishman's death, " continued Cristofano, "my master began to treat me with a coldness and suspicion which increased daily. I was a burden to him, and he was resolved to rid himself of me. I spared him the trouble—quitted Rome— sought the mountains of the Abruzzi— and thence wandered to the fastnesses of Calabria, and became—no matter what. Here I am, Heaven's appointed minister of vengeance. The marchese dies to-night! "

"To-night! old man, " I echoed, horror-stricken. "Add not crime to crime. If he has indeed been guilty of the foul offence you have named, let him be dealt with according to the offended laws of the country. Do not pervert the purposes of justice. "

"Justice! " echoed Cristofano, scornfully.

"Ay, justice. You are poor and powerless, but means may be found to aid you. I will assist the rightful course of vengeance. "

"You shall assist it. I have sworn he shall die before dawn, and the hand to strike the blow shall be yours."

"Mine! never! "

"Your own life will be the penalty of your obstinacy, if you refuse; nor will your refusal save him. By the Mother of Heaven, he dies! and by your hand. You saw how he was struck by your resemblance to the young Englishman this morning in the chiesa. It is wonderful! I know not who or what you are; but to me you are an instrument of vengeance, and as such I shall use you. The blow dealt by you will seem the work of retribution; and I care not if you strike twice, and make my heart your second mark. "

Ere I could reply he called to his comrades, and in a few moments we were speeding across the campagna.

We arrived at a high wall: the old man conducted us to a postern-gate, which he opened. We entered a garden filled with orange-trees, the perfume of which loaded the midnight air. We heard the splash of a fountain at a distance, and the thrilling notes of a nightingale amongst some taller trees. The moon hung like a lamp over the belvidere of the proud villa. We strode along a wide terrace edged by a marble balustrade. The old man pointed to an open summer-house terminating the walk, and gave me a significant look, but he spoke not. A window thrown open admitted us to the house. We were within a hall crowded with statues, and traversed noiselessly its marble floors. Passing through several chambers, we then mounted to a corridor, and entered an apartment which formed the ante-room to another beyond it. Placing his finger upon his lips, and making a sign to his comrades, Cristofano opened a door and disappeared. There was a breathless pause for a few minutes, during which I listened intently but caught only a faint sound as of the snapping of a lock.

Presently the old man returned.

"He sleeps, " he said, in a low deep tone to me; "sleeps as his victim slept—sleeps without a dream of remorse; and he shall awaken, as she awoke, to despair. Come into his chamber! "

We obeyed. The door was made fast within side.

The curtains of the couch were withdrawn, and the moonlight streamed full upon the face of the sleeper. He was hushed in profound repose. No visions seemed to haunt his peaceful slumbers. Could guilt sleep so soundly? I half doubted the old man's story.

Placing us within the shadow of the canopy, Cristofano approached the bed. A stiletto glittered in his hand. "Awake! " he cried, in a voice of thunder.

The sleeper started at the summons.

I watched his countenance. He read Cristofano's errand in his eye. But he quailed not. "Cowardly assassin! " he cried, "you have well consulted your own safety in stealing on my sleep. "

"And who taught me the lesson? " fiercely interrupted the old man. "Am I the first that have stolen on midnight slumber? Gaze upon this? When and how did it acquire its dye? " And he held forth a glove, which looked blackened and stained in the moonlight.

The marchese groaned aloud.

"My cabinet broken open! " at length he exclaimed—"villain! how dared you do this? But why do I rave? I know with whom I have to deal. " Uttering these words he sprung from his couch, with the intention of grappling with the old man; but Cristofano retreated, and at that instant the brigands, who rushed to his aid, thrust me forward. I was face to face with the marchese.

The apparition of the murdered man could not have staggered him more. His limbs were stiffened by the shock, and he remained in an attitude of freezing terror.

"Is he come for vengeance? " he ejaculated.

"He is! " cried Cristofano. "Give him the weapon! " And a stiletto was thrust into my hand. But I heeded not the steel. I tore open my bosom—a small diamond cross was within the folds.

"Do you recollect this? " I demanded of the marchese.

"It was my wife's!" he shrieked, in amazement.

"It was upon the infant's bosom as he slept by her side on that fatal night," said Cristofano. "I saw it sparkle there."

"That infant was myself—that wife my mother!" I cried.

"The murderer stands before you! Strike!" exclaimed Cristofano.

I raised the dagger. The marchese stirred not. I could not strike.

"Do you hesitate?" angrily exclaimed Cristofano.

"He has not the courage," returned the younger Calabrian. "You reproached me this morning with want of filial duty. Behold how a son can avenge his father!"

And he plunged his stiletto within the bosom of the marchese.

"Your father is not yet avenged, young man!" cried Cristofano, in a terrible tone. "You alone can avenge him!"

Ere I could withdraw its point the old man had rushed upon the dagger which I held extended in my grasp.

He fell without a single groan.

THE END

CPSIA information can be obtained
at www.ICGtesting.com
Printed in the USA
BVHW031200280323
661285BV00015B/1263